Elephants Aloft

Written by

KATHI APPELT

Illustrated by

KEITH BAKER

Harcourt Brace & Company

SAN DIEGO   NEW YORK   LONDON

For Katherine

—K. A.

For Babar and Celeste
and all the travelers
in the world

—K. B.

Library of Congress Cataloging-in-Publication Data
Appelt, Kathi, 1954–
Elephants aloft/Kathi Appelt; illustrations by Keith
Baker.
p.   cm.
Summary: Using prepositions, relates the adventures
of two elephants as they travel to Africa to visit their
Auntie Rwanda.
ISBN 0-15-225384-X
[1. Elephants—Fiction. 2. English language—
Prepositions—Fiction.]
I. Baker, Keith, 1953–   ill. II. Title.
PZ7.A6455El   1993
[E]—dc20   92-4231

First edition
A B C D E

Printed in Singapore

The illustrations in this book were done in Liquitex
acrylics on illustration board.
The text and display type was set in ITC Goudy
Sans Bold.
Composition by Thompson Type, San Diego, California
Color separations by Bright Arts, Ltd., Singapore
Production supervision by Warren Wallerstein and
Cheryl Kennedy
Designed by Michael Farmer

Dear Rama and Raja,
I miss you!
Please come
for a visit
Love
Auntie Rwanda

Rama and Raja
ASIA

Rwanda
AFRICA

In

above

beside

through

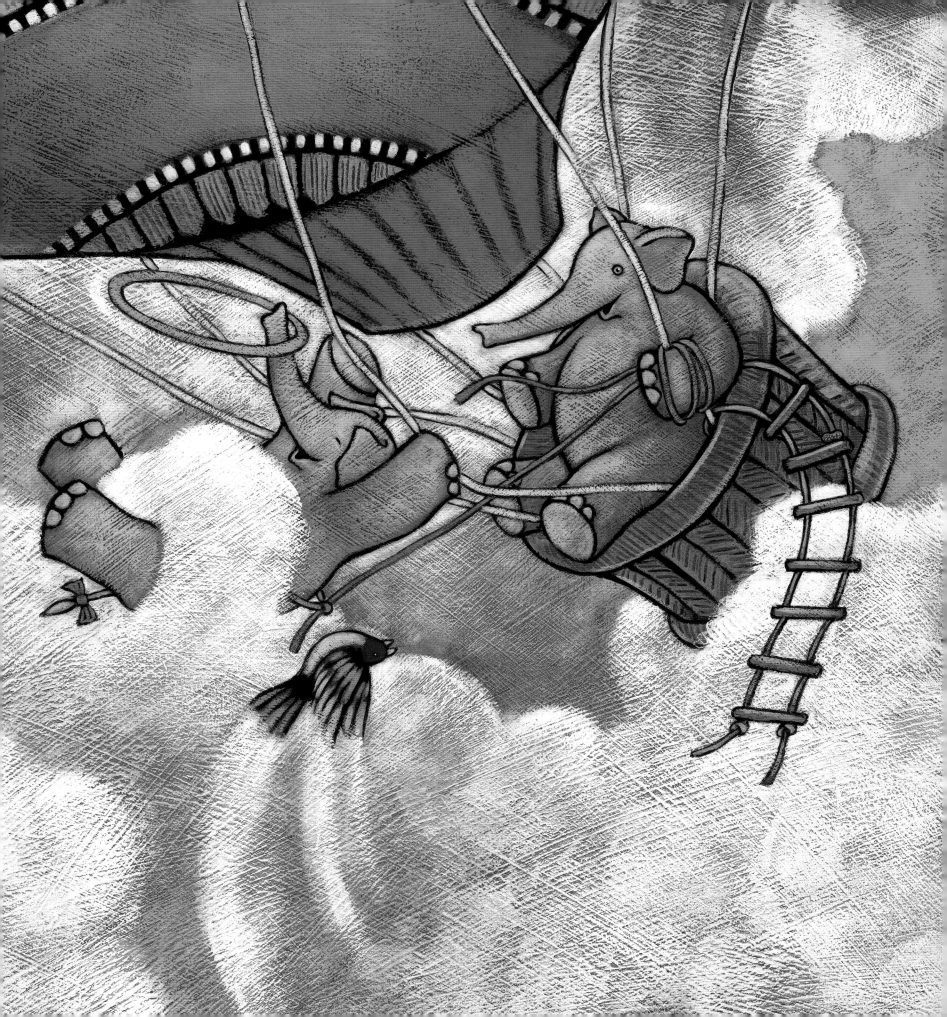

between

behind

across

below

around

under

beyond

over

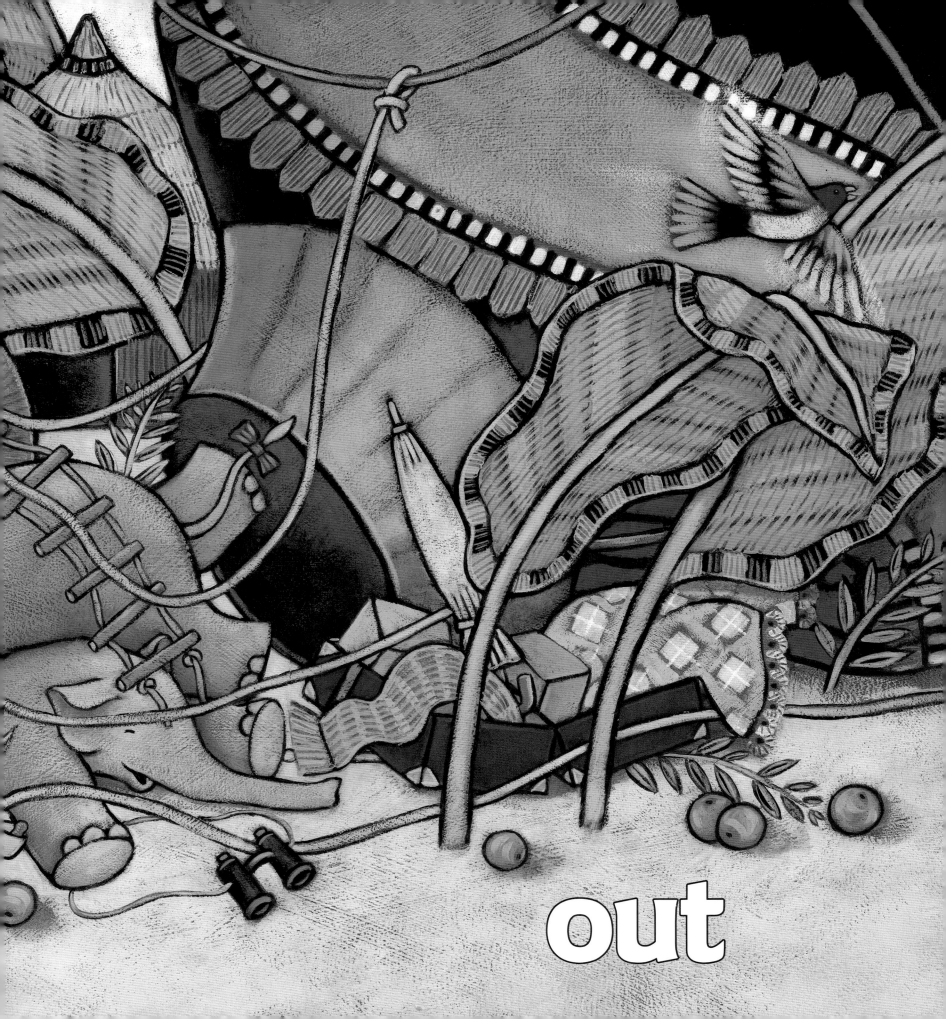

out

and into the arms

of Auntie Rwanda.